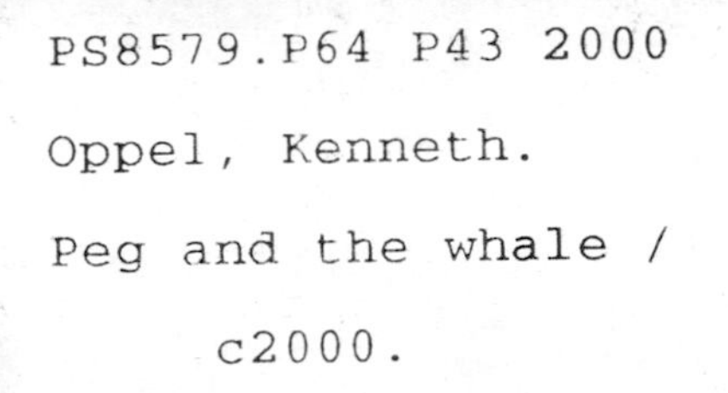
PS8579.P64 P43 2000
Oppel, Kenneth.
Peg and the whale /
c2000.

P9-CCY-541

PEG AND THE WHALE
Copyright © 2000 by Kenneth Oppel.
Illustrations copyright © 2000 by Terry Widener

All rights reserved.

No part of this book may be used or reproduced in any manner whatsoever without prior written permission except in the case of brief quotations embodied in reviews. For information address HarperCollins Publishers Ltd, 55 Avenue Road, Suite 2900, Toronto, Ontario, Canada M5R 3L2.

http://www.harpercanada.com

HarperCollins books may be purchased for educational, business, or sales promotional use. For information please write: Special Markets Department, HarperCollins Canada, 55 Avenue Road, Suite 2900, Toronto, Ontario, Canada M5R 3L2.

First HarperCollins hardcover ed. ISBN 0-00-225497-2
First HarperCollins trade paper ed. ISBN 0-00-648056-X

Canadian Cataloguing in Publication Data

Oppel, Kenneth
Peg and the whale

ISBN 0-00-225497-2
I. Widener, Terry. II. Title.

PS8579.P64P43 2000 jC813'.54 C99-932544-2
PZ7.O614Pe 2000

00 01 02 03 04 05 6 5 4 3 2 1

Book design by Jennifer Reyes
The text for this book is set in Adobe Caslon.
The illustrations are rendered in acrylic on paper.
Printed in Hong Kong

To Sophia and Nathaniel —K. O.

For my sister Pat —T. W.

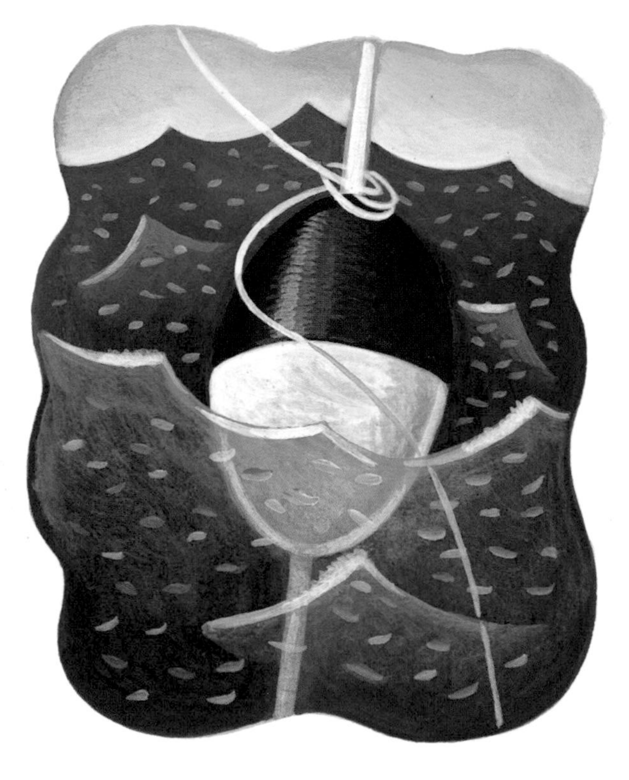

170301

Peg AND THE Whale

By Kenneth Oppel

Illustrated by Terry Widener

HarperCollins*PublishersLtd*

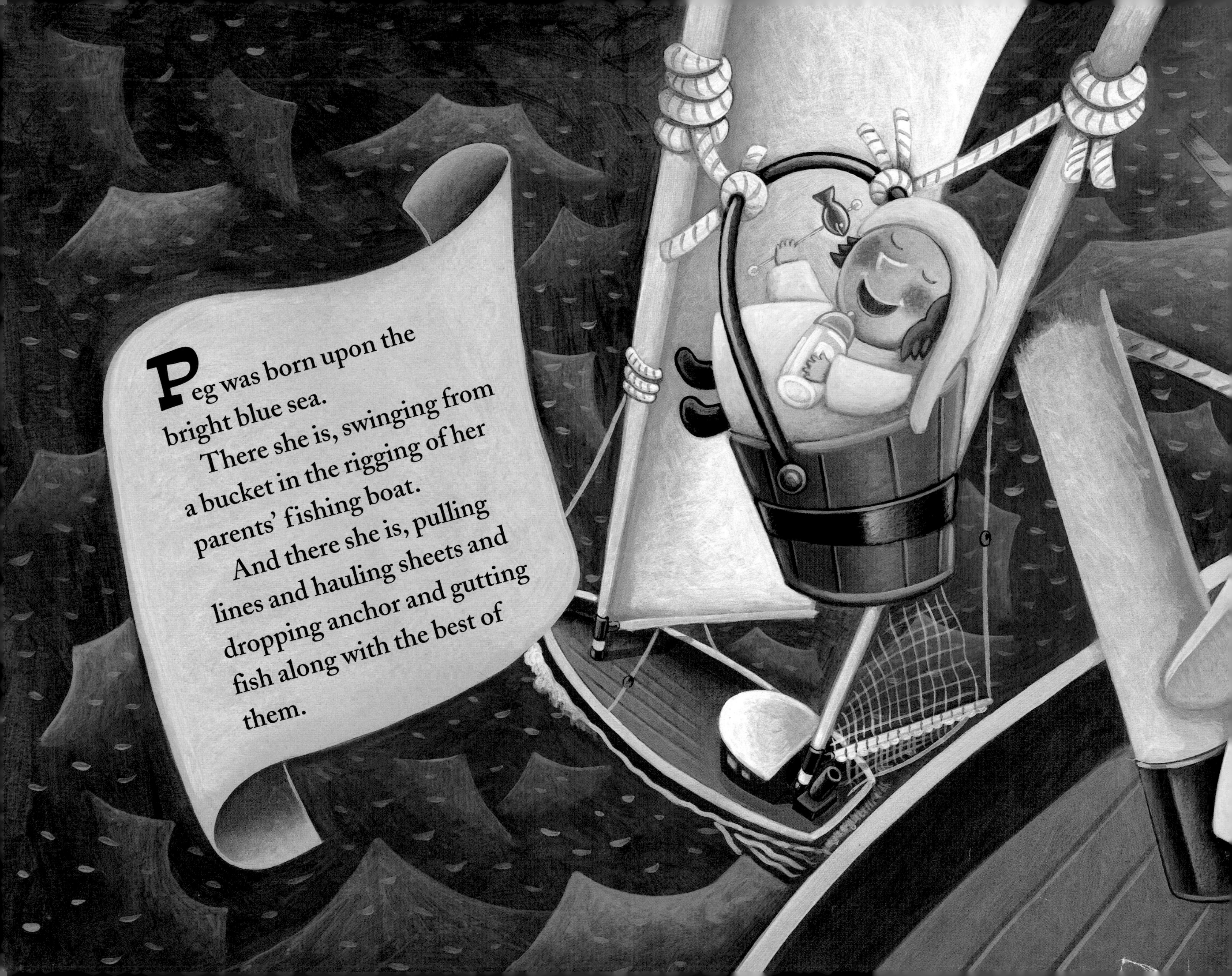

Peg was born upon the bright blue sea.

There she is, swinging from a bucket in the rigging of her parents' fishing boat.

And there she is, pulling lines and hauling sheets and dropping anchor and gutting fish along with the best of them.

A big, strapping lass, Peg was, and she wasn't one to do things in half measures. Anything she turned her hand to she was good at.

But she wanted more than that. She wanted big, she wanted better, she wanted best.

She wanted to be the
WORLD'S BEST FISHERMAN

Now, she'd caught pretty much every fish that swam. She'd hooked herring, halibut, haddock, and hagfish. She'd hauled smelt, sole, sculpin, stickleback, and sturgeon. She'd caught a shark once, but threw it back because it was too small.

But Peg had her sights set higher, you see. She wanted to catch something really big. She wanted to catch herself a whale.

"A whale," her father said, "is not a fish, Peg. It's a mammal."

But Peg would have none of that foolishness. "If it swims and spends more time in water than out, it's a fish. And I'm going to catch me one."

Well, Peg was pushing seven, and she figured it was high time she made something of herself. So one night in harbor she packed up her fishing rod, left her parents a note, and signed on with the whaling ship *Viper*.

The *Viper* shipped out for Labrador that very night. It was big and oily and covered in barnacles. The crew was a mean-looking bunch, and first mate, Bart Maxwell, could curse and spit better than all the others put together.

"I want to catch me a whale," Peg said.

"That right?" said Maxwell. "Can you throw a harpoon?"

"No, but I can hook, bait, and cast a line quicker than you can change your mind."

Bart Maxwell laughed and set her to work swabbing decks.

But Peg had a chance to prove herself the very next morning. There was a stiff wind blowing, and the captain's hat was knocked right off his head into the waves.

"A doubloon for the sailor who gets my hat!" the captain cried.

Bart Maxwell threw the first harpoon and missed the hat by yards.

"Curse the wind!" he shouted.

He threw again, and again he missed.

"A pox on these scurvy harpoons!" he swore, snatching up another.

"I'll do it!" said Peg, bold as can be.

She grabbed her fishing rod and cast her line. The hook sank through the hat first try, and Peg reeled it in.

Bart Maxwell gave her a look that would fry fish.

"Nice trick, my girl," he growled, "but I don't think you'll be catching a whale with that rod of yours."

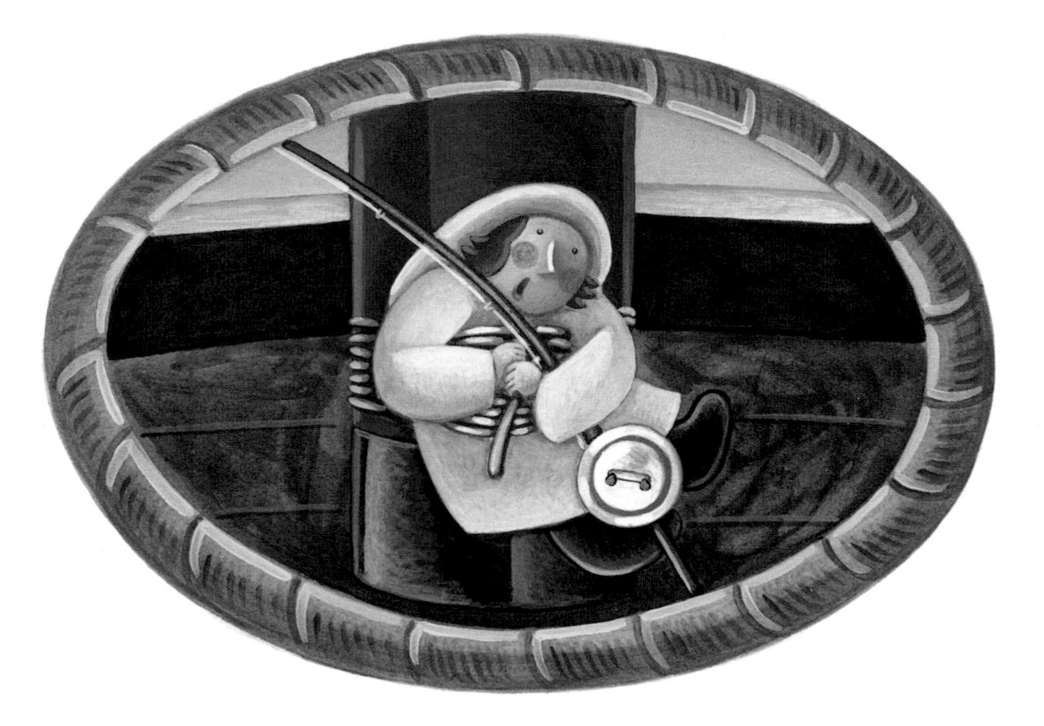

The next day the whale came.

"Thar she blows!" hollered a sailor from the crow's nest.

Before the men could even get to the whaleboats, Peg was at the side with her fishing rod. She swung that rod back over her shoulder and cast with all her might.

The whale took the hook, and the line played out faster than a tune from a jack-in-the-box.

"I've got her!" she shouted.

She tied herself to the ship's mast and held tight.

Well, the mast bent nearly double, and that whale pulled the *Viper* through the ocean on a Nantucket sleigh ride.

"The lass has hooked herself a whale!" the sailors cried in amazement.

"She's reeling it in!" they cried.

"She's reeling in a whale!"

"Nice fishing, girl," said Bart Maxwell, and in a flash he cut the rope holding Peg to the mast.

Peg sailed through the air, hit the water, and went skipping over the waves after the whale, still holding her fishing rod.

"Just as well," she thought. "That old ship was only slowing me down."

Then the whale stopped.
"Ah-ha! Plain tuckered out!" thought Peg, reeling in. "She knows she's met her match!"

The whale turned and came at Peg, big as a blue mountain.
"I've got you!" Peg cried.

Peg got swallowed whole.

There was a tremendous roar of water, and she was spluttering and splashing and tumbling and thrashing right down the whale's gullet and into its stomach.

It was black as a night without moon or stars, only blacker.

Peg lit a waterproof match.

She reckoned there were enough planks and busted beams down there to set up shop as a carpenter. A cod slapped at her feet. Seeing as she felt a bit peckish, she made herself a little fire, hung up her wet clothes to dry, and fried up some fish.

After she'd eaten, she got dressed. She figured the only way out was up. So she took some of that busted-up wood and the thighbone from an old pirate's skeleton, and hammered herself a ladder.

Peg climbed back up the whale's gullet and into its mouth. She felt a big draft coming from overhead. The whale sighed and, *whoosh,* Peg was blasted right up through the blowhole. She reckoned she was about thirty feet in the air before she came back down and landed on the whale's back.

Now she could see what was what.

The *Viper* was nowhere in sight.

"Just as well," Peg thought. "I didn't much care for the crew."

All in all she was mighty pleased. She'd wanted to catch herself a whale and here she'd gone and done it. Riding a whale through the Labrador Sea! But after an hour or so she figured it was probably time to be moving on.

"Whale," she said, "looks like you're my ride back to shore."

But that whale, it had a mind of its own, and took Peg on a tour of the Arctic. Peg kept warm by doing jumping jacks and singing sea shanties. When it got too cold, or the whale decided to dive under the ice, Peg just jumped back down the blowhole and slid into the whale's stomach.

It was damp and a tad smelly, but nothing she wasn't used to. And there were plenty of fresh fish for the eating. She built herself a little bunk to nap in. It was just like home, really. Darnedest thing, if she didn't start feeling a bit fond of that whale.

But Peg was also getting just a mite bored and, if truth be told, a little homesick. Well, she went back to work, sawing and hammering, and made herself the longest rudder in the world to steer that stubborn whale.

Didn't look like much, but it seemed to do the trick.

She got the whale turned back south.

A few days later, Peg caught sight of a ship on the horizon.
The *Viper*?
No, her mother and father's fishing boat!
Peg gave the whale a little pat.
"Good work," she said.

The whale swam alongside the boat, and Peg stepped aboard. She was a bit stiff and frozen round the edges, but none the worse for wear. The whale blew up a big geyser of water and dived down into the sea.

"Peg, we were a little bit worried," her mother said.

"But it looks like you went and caught yourself a whale," said her father.

"Well, you know," Peg said, "a whale is not a fish, so I figured I'd let it go."

"Very good then," said her father.

Peg stayed on fishing for a while, but she was pushing eight, and she figured it was high time she made something of herself. After all, she wanted big, she wanted better, she wanted best.

PROPERTY OF
SENECA COLLEGE
RESOURCE CENTRE
KING CAMPUS

And she thought she'd try her hand at something new.

THE END